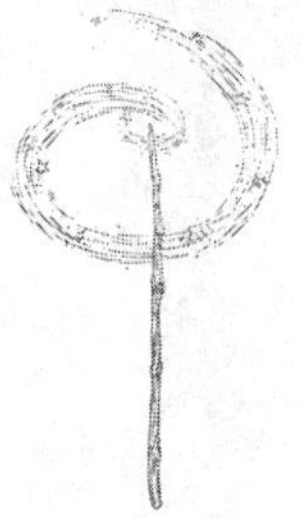

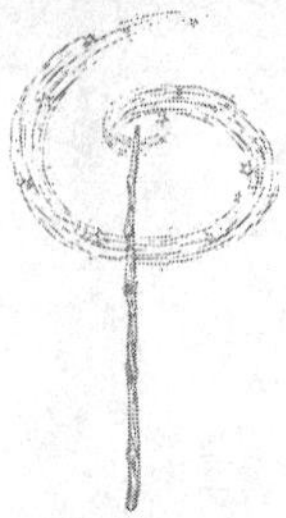

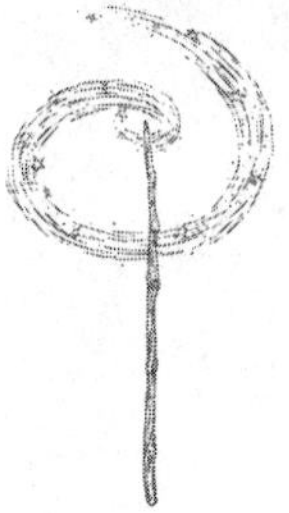

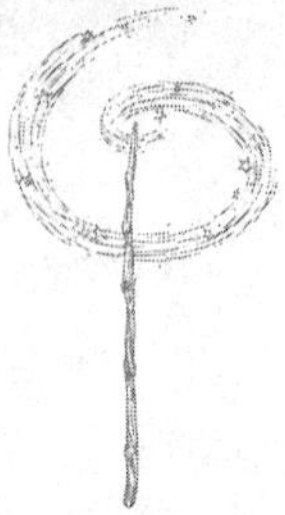

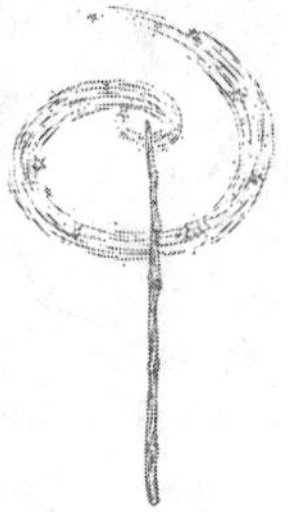

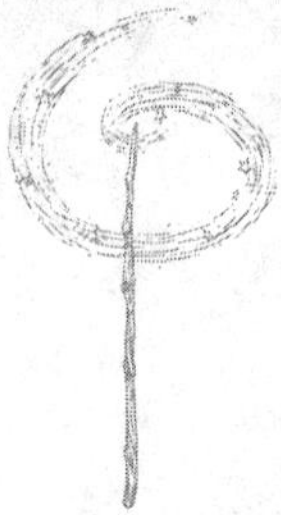

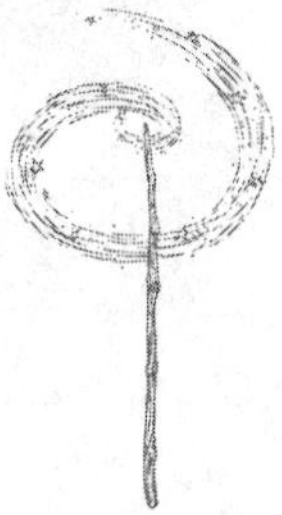

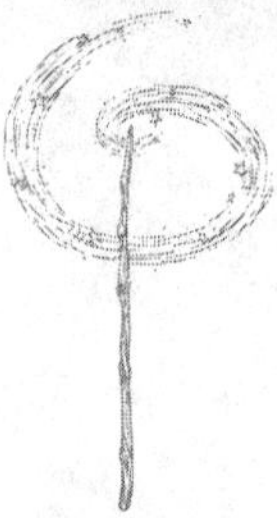

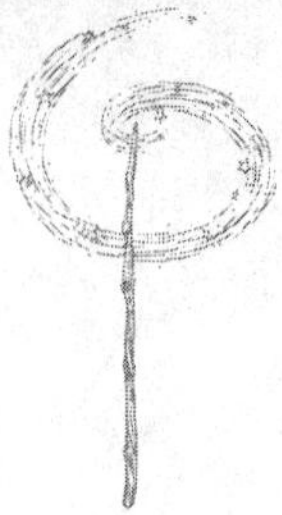

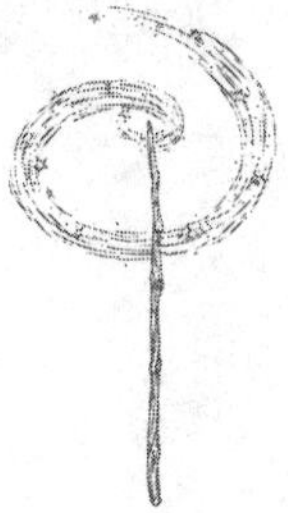

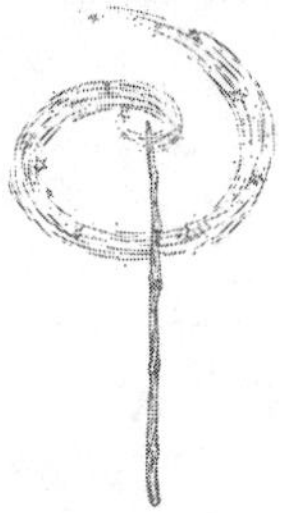

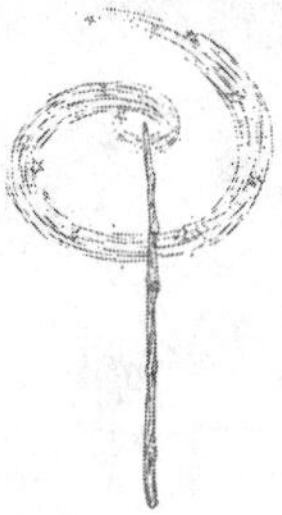

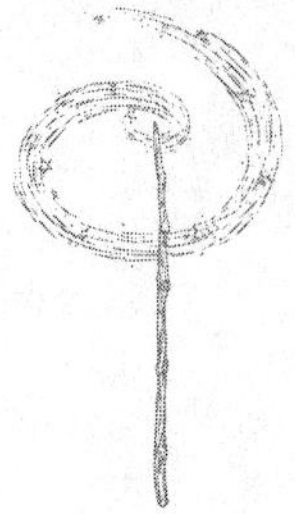

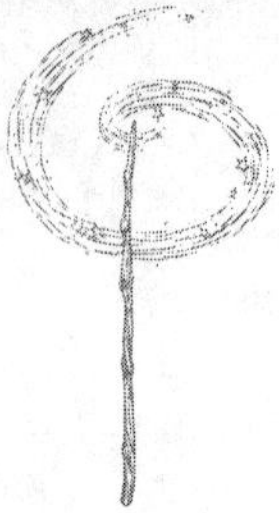

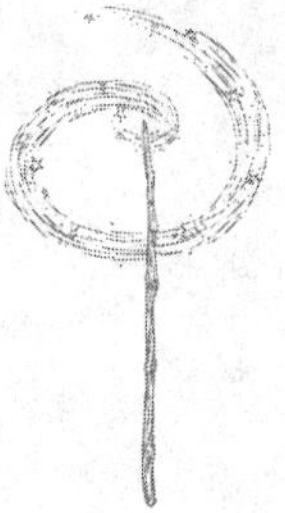

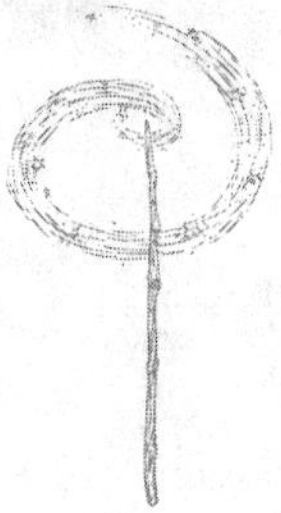

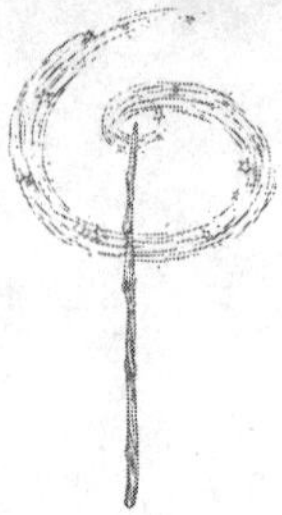

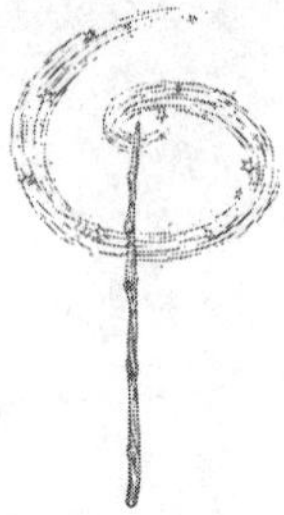

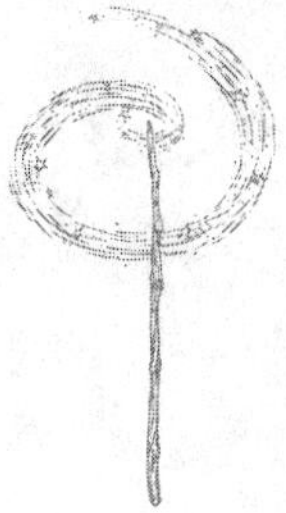

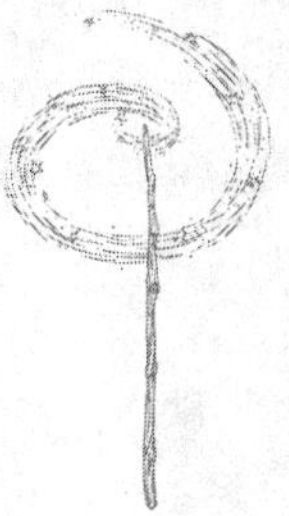

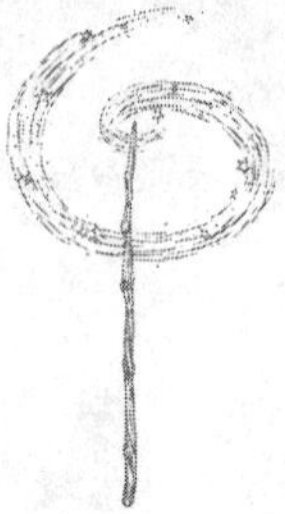

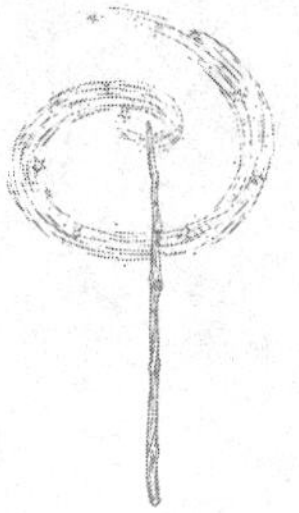

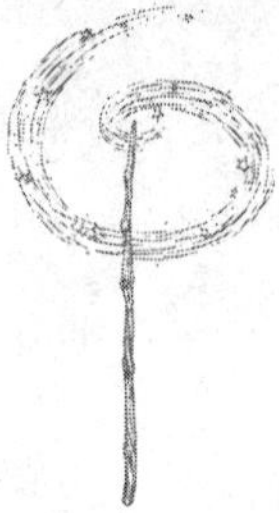

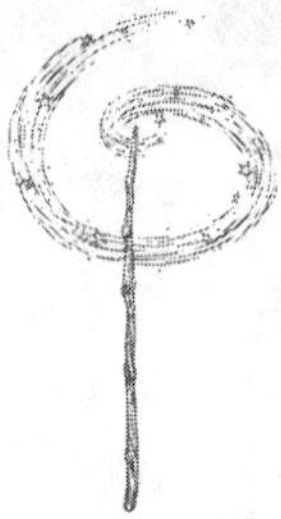

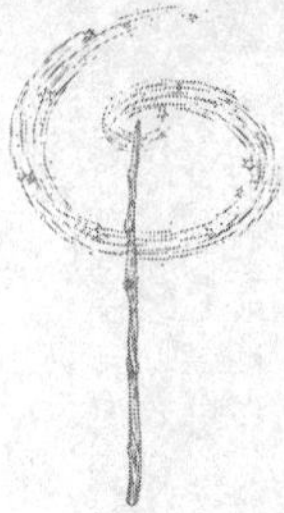

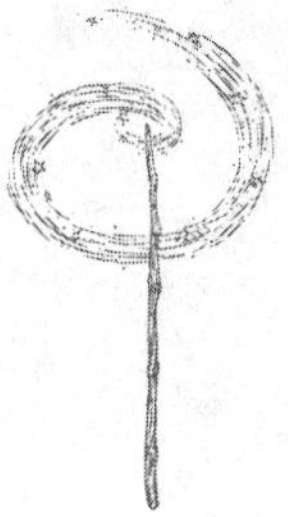

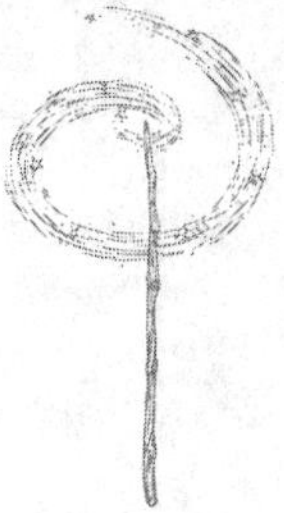

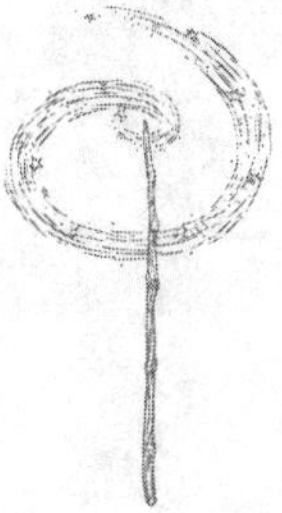

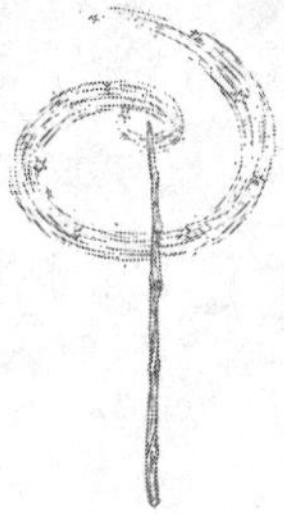

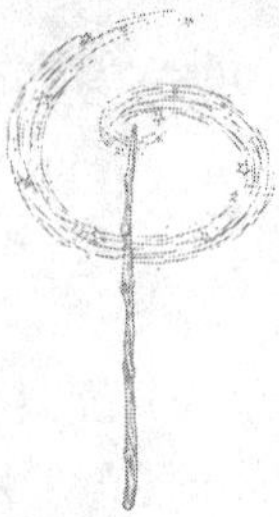

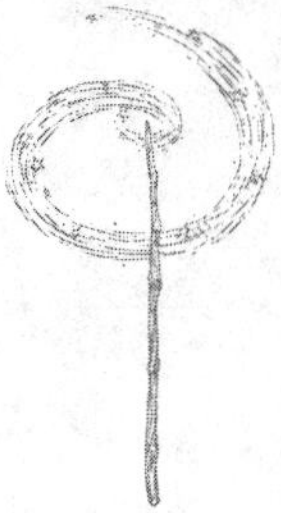

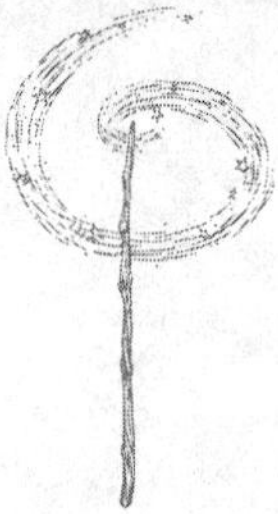

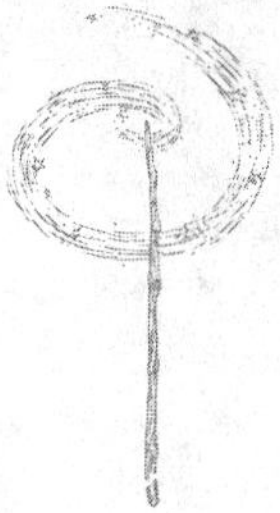

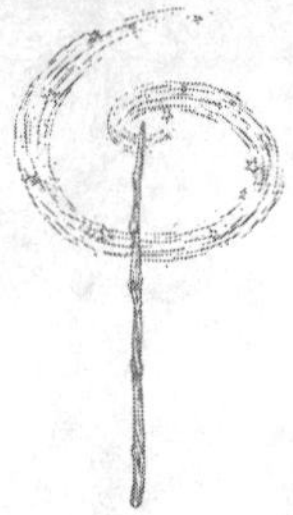

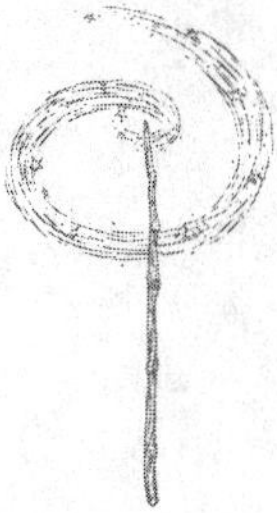

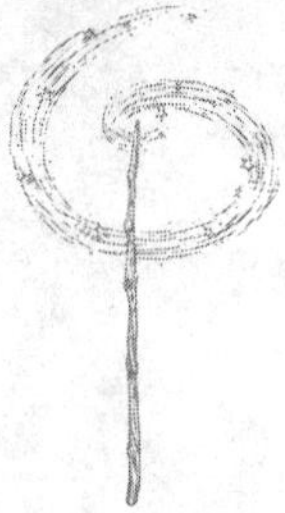

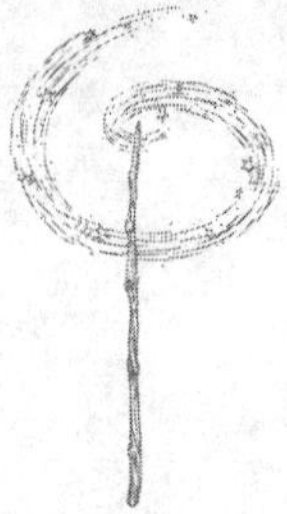

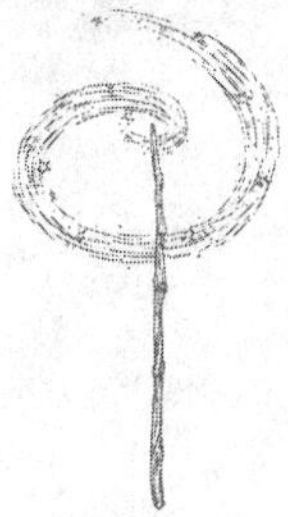

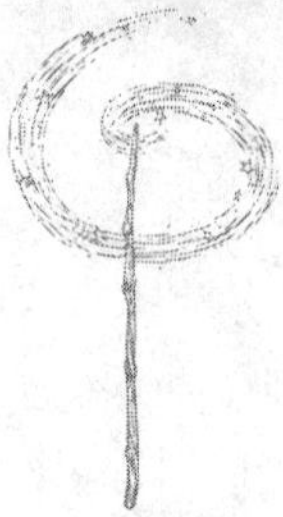

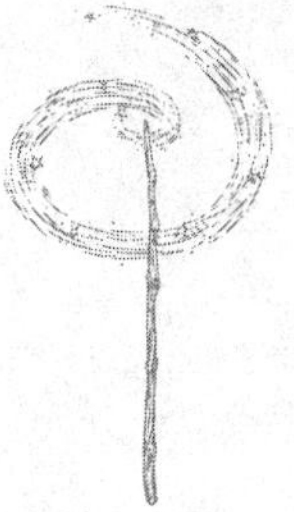

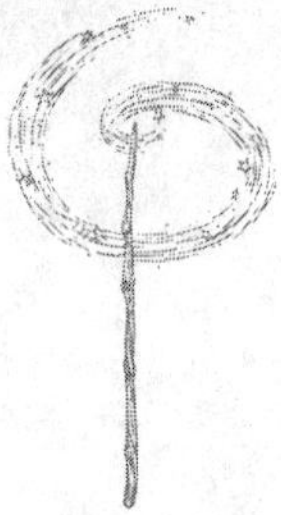

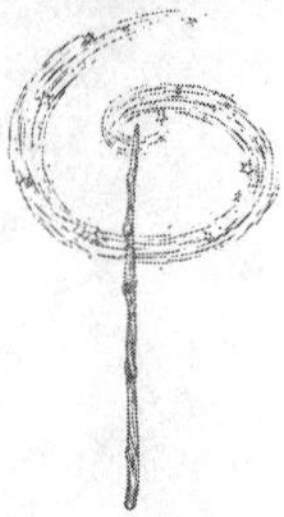

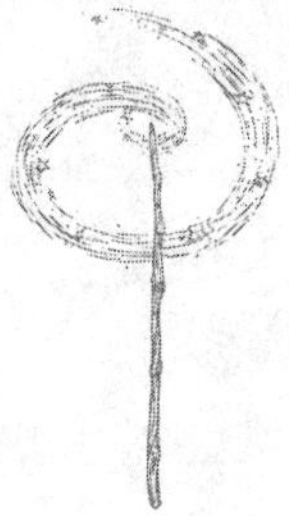

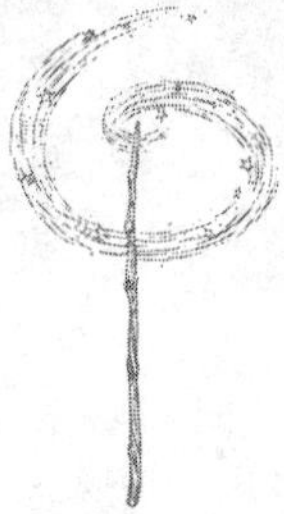

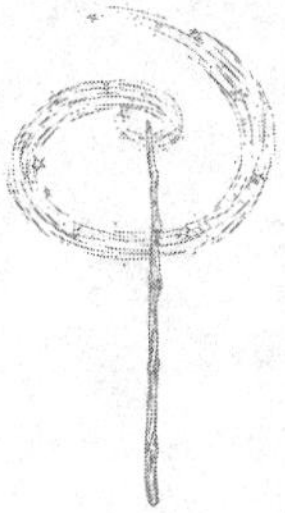

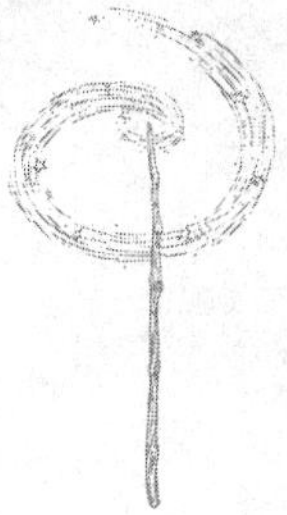

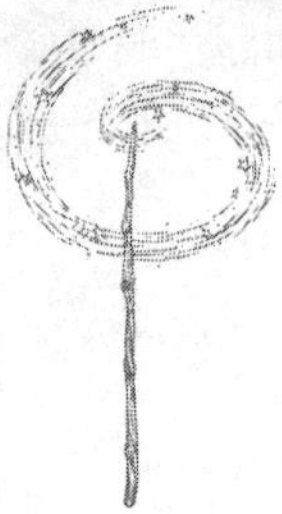

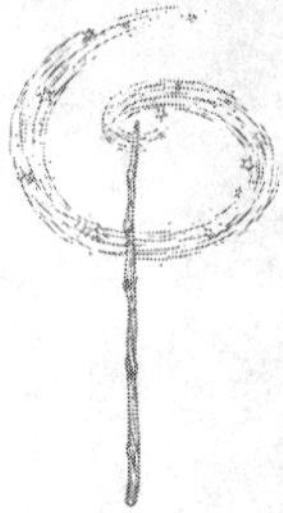

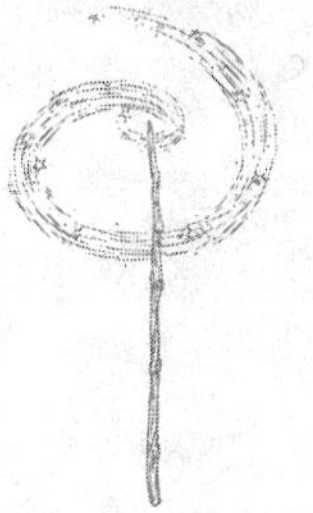

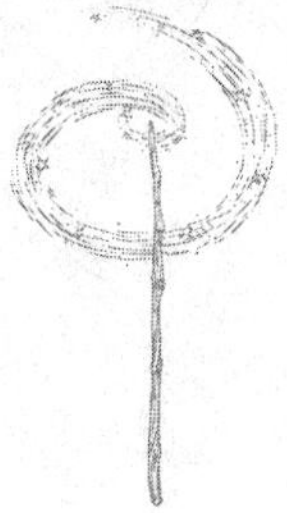

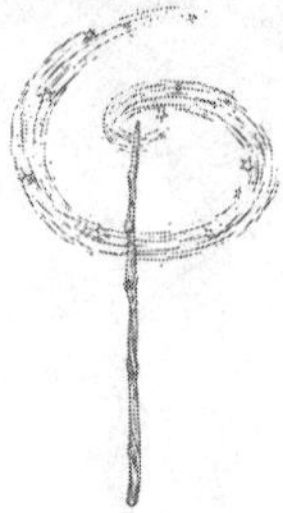

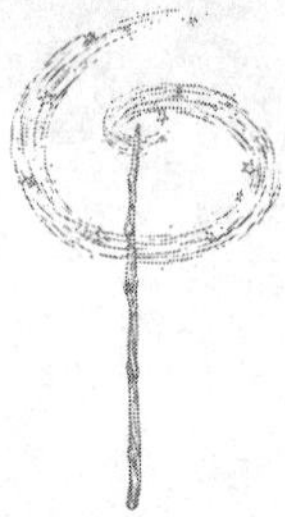

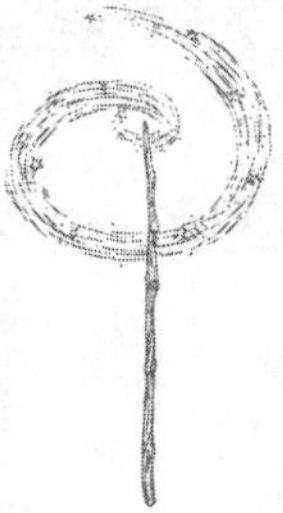

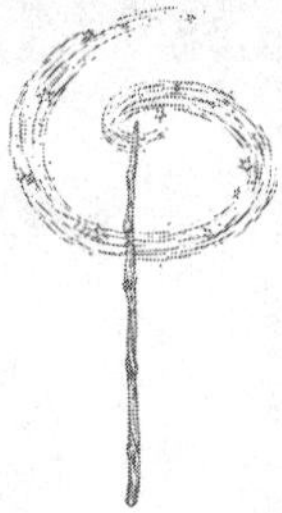

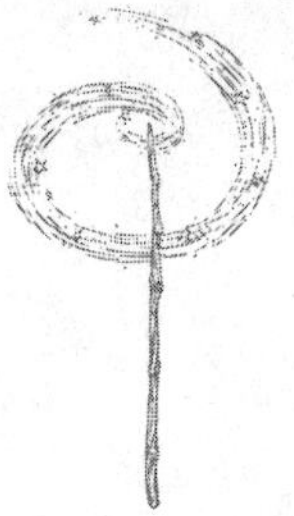

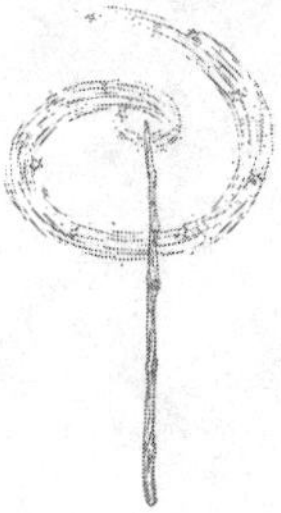

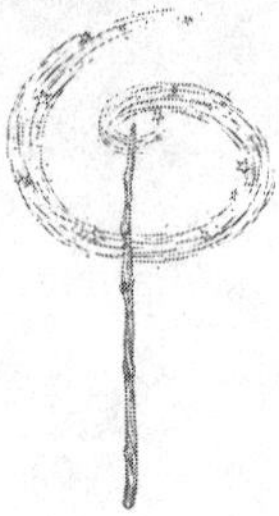

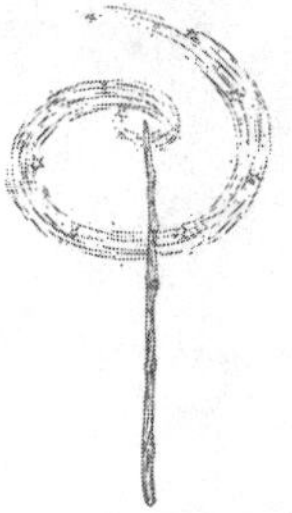

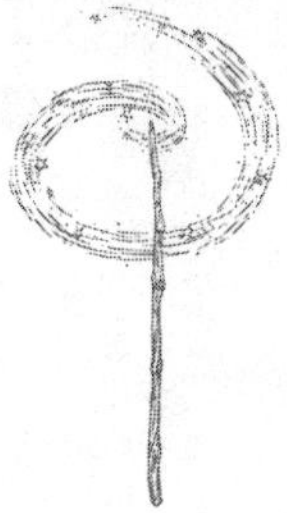

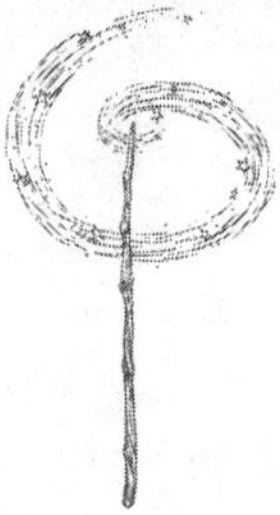

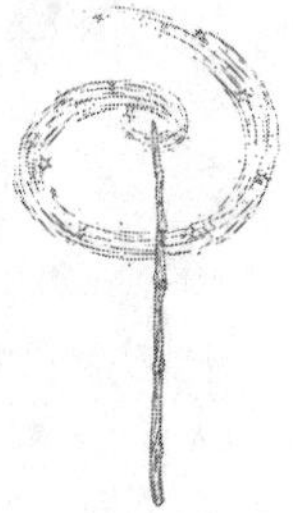

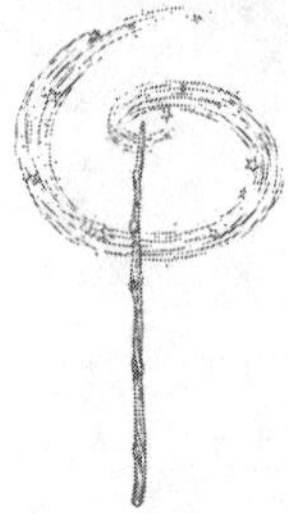

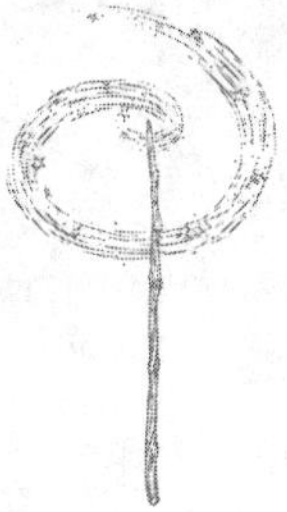

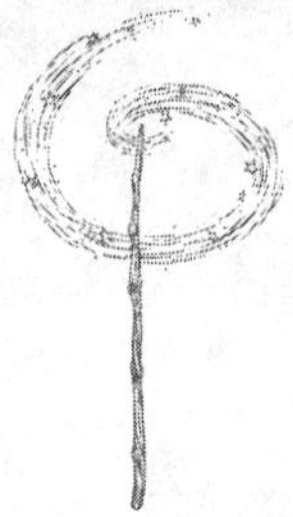

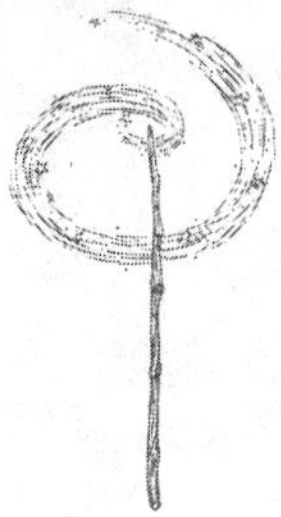

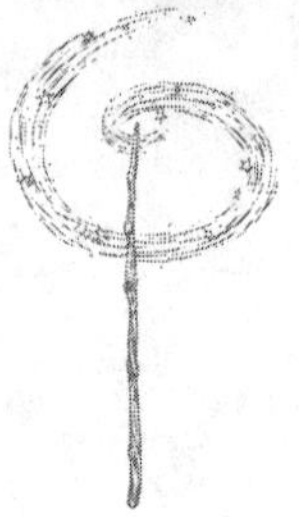

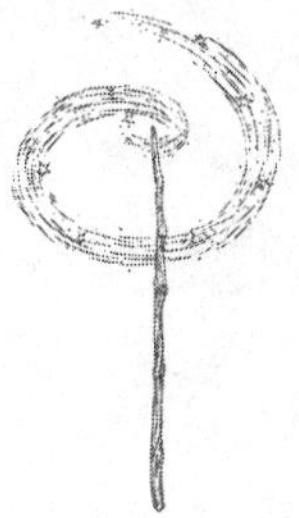

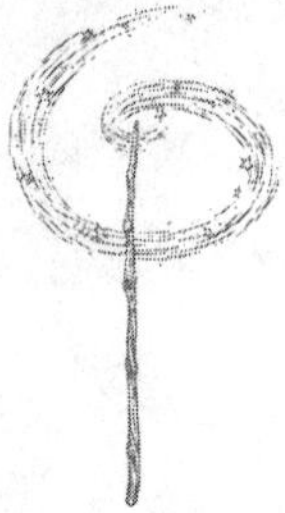

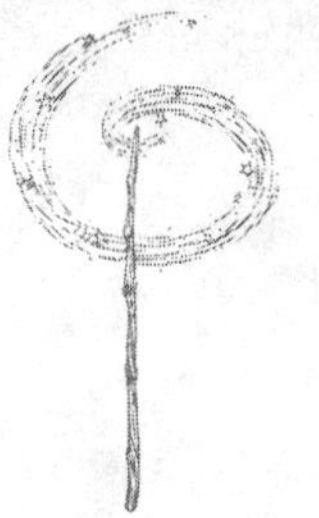

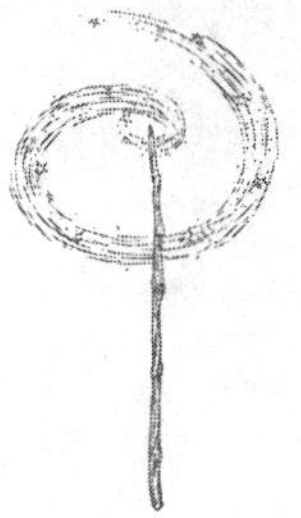

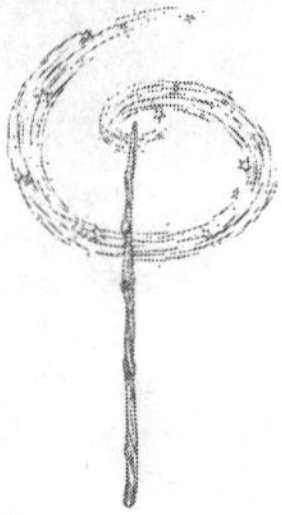

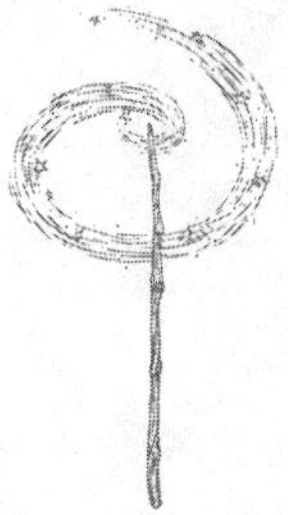

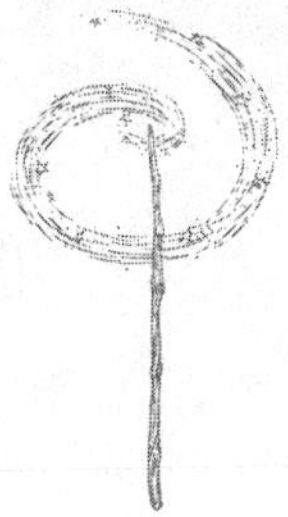

ISBN 0-439-23654-1
Printed in the U.S.A.
First Scholastic printing, November 2000